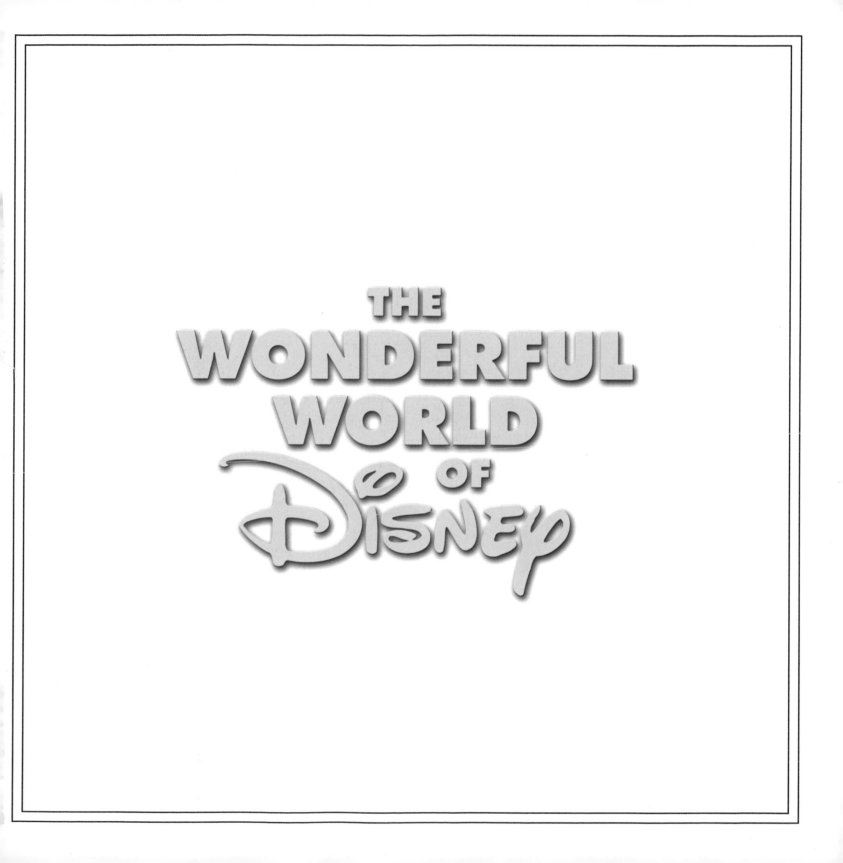

THE WONDERFUL WORLD OF Disney

Disney PRESS

New York

Table of Contents

QUICK CLIPS

CARTOON CORNER

PRESENTING...

It all began on October 27, 1954, when Walt Disney launched his first weekly series called *Disneyland* on ABC. The first few seasons showcased television debuts of Disney feature films and compilations of earlier Disney shorts pieced together with new interstitial footage. The Studio was also committed to producing all-new, original programs.

After several successful seasons, Walt Disney was anxious to move into the relatively new field of color TV. "This is a breakthrough that I have anticipated for years," Walt said. "Pioneering in the color field [is] as thrilling as making the first move in adding sound to our animated films." NBC lured Walt away from ABC because of its superior color-broadcasting quality, and *Walt Disney's Wonderful World of Color* was born on September 24, 1961.

Over the years, the series would change networks several times and the title would undergo many revisions, but the all-time Sunday night family favorite will always be best known as *The Wonderful World of Disney.* In these pages, you will find some of the beloved characters and stories that have appeared on the series and have made their way into the homes and hearts of millions.

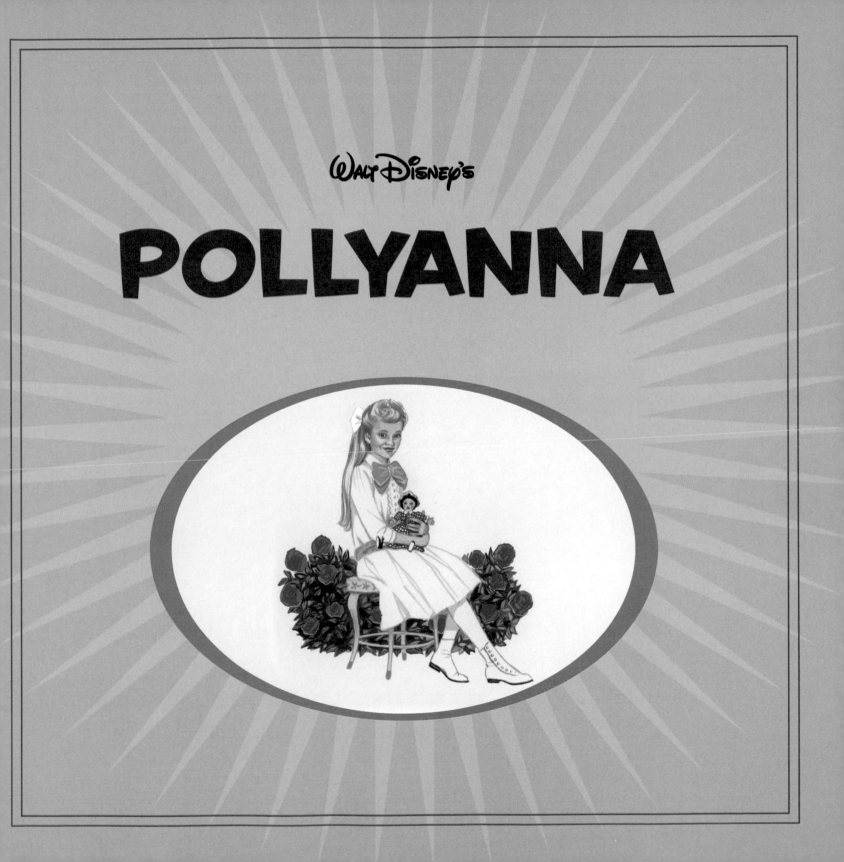

Pollyanna stared around her new room. "I'm glad there isn't a mirror," she said to Nancy, the maid. "I won't have to look at my freckles. I'm glad, too, to have a room of my very own."

"Do you always find something to be glad about?" asked Nancy.

"I try to," said Pollyanna.

Pollyanna was an orphan. She had just come to live with her rich Aunt Polly. Aunt Polly was very strict, but she was good to Pollyanna and bought her many lovely new clothes.

Pollyanna had never owned any brand-new clothes—only hand-me-downs.

One morning, Pollyanna was walking by the orphanage when she saw a boy climbing out of a window. He swung into a tree, then jumped neatly down to the sidewalk.

"I'm Jimmy Bean," he said to Pollyanna. "I'm an orphan."

"So am I," said Pollyanna. "My name is Pollyanna Whittier."

"I'm going fishing," said Jimmy. "Do you want to come along?"

Pollyanna nodded, and away they went to the stream. They had no hook. Instead, they used a tin can tied to a string. They did not catch a single fish, but they still had fun.

On the way home, Jimmy took Pollyanna into a big, overgrown garden. He pointed to a tree in front of a big house. "This is the tallest tree in town," he said. "Be very quiet. Old Man Pendergast lives here, and he hates kids."

Pollyanna was a little scared, but she followed Jimmy over to the tree. "I'm going to climb the tree," said Jimmy. "I bet I can see the whole town from the top." He started to shimmy up the trunk when—*crash!*— a wild-eyed old man burst out of the underbrush. It was Pendergast!

Pendergast tried to grab Pollyanna, but she ducked out of his reach. Jimmy was not so lucky. Pendergast seized him and dragged him into the house.

"Help!" screamed Jimmy.

Pollyanna wanted to run away. But Jimmy was her friend. She had to try to help him.

Bravely, she headed into the house. Pendergast and Jimmy were in the living room. The old man was about to telephone the police.

"You let Jimmy go!" Pollyanna said loudly. "He didn't hurt anything, and neither did I."

Pendergast was so surprised that he let go of the boy. Jimmy dashed for the door, and disappeared quickly before the old man could catch him.

Pendergast glared at Pollyanna. "Go on. Get out of here!" he bellowed.

Pollyanna started to go, then stopped short. On the wall were stunning patches of colored light.

"What a beautiful rainbow!" she said with a gasp.

"That's not a rainbow," hissed Pendergast. "It's the sun shining through the prisms of the lamp."

"I like to think it's a rainbow," said Pollyanna. Then she added, "Maybe you're not glad I came here, but I am." And she skipped merrily out of the room.

A few days later, Pollyanna and Nancy brought baskets of food to some of the poor families in town. The last basket was for old Mrs. Snow.

Mrs. Snow was very cranky. She found fault with everything and everybody—even Pollyanna.

But Pollyanna only laughed, and showed Mrs. Snow how to make rainbows on the wall with the glass from her lamp.

One day, the townspeople decided to hold a big fair to raise money for a new orphanage. Pollyanna did all she could to help. She even asked Old Man Pendergast to take a booth and sell glass pendants.

"We'll call them rainbow-makers," said Pollyanna.

And Mrs. Snow promised to make a quilt.

That afternoon when Dr. Chilton, the town doctor, ran into Aunt Polly, he told her about the fair.

"We don't need a new orphanage," she said with a scowl. "I'll pay for repairs on the old one."

"The people do not want your charity," replied Dr. Chilton. "They want to raise the money themselves."

This made Aunt Polly very angry. When she returned home, she told Pollyanna, "You stay away from that fair."

"But they're going to have a parade," said Pollyanna, "and free corn on the cob, and ice cream and—"

"You're not going, and that's the end of it!" snapped Aunt Polly.

But Pollyanna did go.

Jimmy Bean helped her climb down the big tree outside her attic window. They were so quiet, Aunt Polly did not hear them.

At the fair, Pollyanna and Jimmy ate ice cream, watermelon, taffy apples, and corn on the cob.

And Pollyanna won a beautiful doll at the fishpond booth.

"Am I glad!" she cried. "I never had a doll of my own before!"

When Pollyanna got home, she climbed back up the tree easily. But as she jumped over to the windowsill, she slipped and fell to the ground. Aunt Polly heard Pollyanna scream and hurried outside.

Pollyanna was lying very, very still.

"She is badly hurt," Aunt Polly told Nancy. "Call Dr. Chilton! And hurry!"

The next day, Dr. Chilton told Pollyanna that her legs had been hurt, and that she had to go to the hospital.

"I won't go," said Pollyanna. "I'll never get well. And I'll never be glad again in my whole life, either."

Aunt Polly was sad when she heard this. She loved Pollyanna very much—and she was not the only one. Pollyanna had won the love of everyone in town. That afternoon, they all came to see her, including Jimmy and Pendergast.

"Mr. Pendergast has adopted me," said Jimmy.

"Oh, I'm so glad!" cried Pollyanna. She thought for a moment. Then she smiled. "I will go to the hospital, Aunt Polly—and I'll get well for you and all my friends."

And she did!

Big Red was a beautiful red setter.

He was not a house dog or a pet dog. He was a show dog and lived in the kennels of a very rich man.

His master looked after him carefully, because he wanted Big Red to win first prize in dog shows.

Every day Big Red was brushed and combed. He had lots to eat and went for walks every day.

But Big Red was unhappy, because he did not have a friend to play with. He did not belong to anybody.

Then one day a boy came to the kennels. His name was René. And he and Big Red became friends.

Now René brushed Big Red's fine coat. He fed Big Red and took him for walks.

René and Big Red played games together.
They played walking-along-a-log.

They played jumping-across-the-stream.

They played chasing-around-the-tree.

And in the evenings, they sat quietly together while René played a song on his harmonica.

René and Big Red were good friends.

But Big Red was still a show dog.

And one day, his master said, "Big Red, you are not a house dog. You are not a pet dog. You are a show dog. And tomorrow you must go to the big city."

Sadly, Big Red sat in his cage in the train.

A kind guard let Big Red out of his cage.

"There you are, boy—stretch those fine long legs," said the guard. "I'll get you some water."

Suddenly, the train went around a curve. The doors of Big Red's car slid open.

Big Red jumped out!

"That is the end of Big Red," said his master when he heard the terrible news.

René was sad. Big Red was his friend.

"Big Red does not know how to hunt," the master explained. "He is a show dog. He cannot live in the wild woods."

"I will find him. I must find him," said René.

"You will never find him," said the master. "The woods are big and wild. And you, too, will get lost."

"My uncle taught me many things about the woods," said René. "I will go there and look for Big Red."

René got on the train—the same train that had carried Big Red.

"You will never find him, son," said the same kind guard.

Suddenly, the train went around a curve. And René saw that the train slowed down.

"Perhaps *this* is where he jumped off," said René. And René jumped off, too.

René wondered which way to go. Then he saw a stream. Perhaps Big Red drank some water here, he thought.

René walked along the bank. And sure enough, there was a footprint! "It's a dog's footprint!" René exclaimed. "It must be Big Red's!"

René walked and walked, but there were no more footprints. It began to grow dark.

Suddenly, René stopped. His sharp eyes had noticed something caught on a thistle. It was a piece of red hair—Big Red's hair!

"Big Red, Big Red!" called René.

But there was no answering bark.

Now the sun was setting. Sadly, René unrolled his blanket and lay down.

As soon as morning came, René set off again.

"Big Red, Big Red!" he called.

But there was still no answering bark.

René walked and walked.

A while later, he saw a patch of grass that lay flat. Perhaps Big Red had slept there.

"Big Red! Big Red!" called René.

But his voice sounded small in the tall mountains.

René sat down under a tree to rest.

He pulled out his harmonica and began to play a sad little tune.

The music rose sweet and clear in the mountain air. It rose above the treetops. It drifted softly down the valley to a quiet pool.

And Big Red, drinking by the pool, lifted his head.

For a moment the dog stood still, one paw raised as he listened intently.

And then he gave a loud bark and began to run.

"Big Red, Big Red!" called René. He had heard the bark. He began
running. He saw a flash of red in the bushes—it was Big Red! It really was!
René laughed and cheered.

Big Red leaped at René and barked with joy.

"Big Red, you old clown!" René cried. "I came to find you, and you found me!"

And then René looked more closely at the dog.

"You are thin and hungry, Big Red," he said. "Come, I must take you back to your master."

When the master saw René and the dog, he could hardly believe his eyes.
"I never thought I would see either of you again," the master said.

"He found me, sir," said René quietly.

"Then he is yours, René," replied the master. "He loves you, and you love him. You belong together."

And so, at last, Big Red was not just a show dog.

At last, he really belonged to somebody.

And at last, Big Red was happy.

"Being shipwrecked is fun!" yelled Francis Robinson, as he slid down the slippery deck.

His mother shuddered. Only the day before, the family had been

snug and safe on the ship that was carrying them to a new home.

But then came the storm. The ship had run aground on the rocks. And now the Swiss family was alone on the shipwrecked vessel.

"Our only hope is that island," said the father. "We must build a raft and get to it."

"Perhaps we'll find buried treasure," said Ernst Robinson hopefully.

"And pirates," added Francis.

The father and his two elder sons, Fritz and Ernst, set to work.

At last the raft was ready.

"Now, tie the animals so that they will float along behind us," said the father.

"Can the chickens and the cow and pig swim?" asked Francis.

"These empty kegs will float in the water and hold them up," explained Fritz.

Ernst grinned. "I'll bet we're the first castaways to land with our own fresh milk and egg supply!"

"Don't forget Duke and Turk!" cried Francis. The two big dogs wagged their tails. They were ready to leap aboard the raft.

"No," said the father. "The family first, then the things we really need. After that, we'll see about the dogs."

But Francis had other ideas. When his father turned away, Francis quietly beckoned the dogs.

They swam after the raft, and when the Swiss family landed on the island, the two big dogs were with them.

It was a beautiful island.

"See," said Fritz. "The sand is as white as the snow at home."

"Oh, there are monkeys, too!" exclaimed Francis. "I'll have a monkey for a pet!"

"Look at those big coconut palms," said Ernst.

"And here," said the father, "is a big tree to shelter us from the rain."

"—and from wild animals," added the mother.

The father, Fritz, and Ernst set to work to build a tree house, high in the thick branches.

They made many trips to the wrecked ship, for they needed planks and nails and tools.

"Getting these heavy planks up into the tree is the hardest part," said Fritz.

His father nodded. "The house will take longer to build than I thought."

"What we need is an elephant," said Francis. "They're very strong."

The others laughed.

When part of the flooring was finished, Francis was allowed to climb up.

"But just to make sure you don't fall, we'll tie this rope around your waist," said Ernst.

They tied the other end to a strong branch.

"Now, I can catch my monkey," said Francis. There were many monkeys in the branches. His father and brothers were too busy to notice him crawl out on a branch. Near the end sat a solemn-faced little monkey with big brown eyes.

"Here, monk! Here, monk!" called Francis.

But the monkey backed away.

Francis followed, reaching for the monkey's paw. Then the animal suddenly screeched and swung by its tail to another branch.

Francis was so startled, he fell out of the tree!

The rope around his waist stopped him a foot or two above the ground.

"Francis, Francis, are you all right?" His mother ran to him as Ernst cut the rope at the top. Francis jumped to the ground.

"No more tree climbing for you till the house is finished," said his mother.

Bored and unhappy and munching on a stick of sugarcane, Francis wandered off into the jungle.

He came to a wide clearing, and suddenly he stopped. There, nibbling on some young branches, stood a baby elephant!

Francis moved a little closer. "Here, little elephant," he cooed.

He held out his stick of sugarcane, and the elephant stretched out its trunk.

Carefully, Francis untied the rope from around his waist and made a noose. The elephant stepped into the noose, and Francis yanked it tight.

"Oh," said Francis happily. "I never knew anyone who had a baby elephant for a pet!"

Suddenly, the elephant trumpeted shrilly and tried to free itself.

It was then that Francis saw a tiger. The big beast was crouching in the bushes, ready to spring.

"Go away! Scat!" yelled Francis. He picked up a rock and threw it.

At that moment, the two big dogs, Duke and Turk, burst into the clearing. Behind them came Francis's mother. She clung tightly to Francis as the two dogs went after the tiger.

Outnumbered, the big cat shook itself free of the dogs and disappeared into the jungle.

"Oh, you wonderful, wonderful dogs!" cried the mother, hugging them.

"They sure showed that old tiger who was boss!" said Francis proudly.

"Francis," said his mother sternly, "you might have been killed, wandering off like that!"

Francis hung his head. "I'm sorry, Mother. I didn't mean to scare you. But—" He looked longingly at the elephant. "But—please, couldn't I keep him?"

His mother sighed. "All right, Francis," she said. "If you promise to look after him yourself."

"Oh, boy!" yelled Francis. "A real elephant of my very own!"

Proudly, Francis led the elephant back to where his father and brothers were building the tree house.

"Look, Father. I found an elephant to help us build the tree house!" he exclaimed.

The father smiled and went back to hauling planks with Fritz and Ernst.

Francis stood close to the elephant's big ear.

"It's a game," he whispered. "You pick up that plank, and then I'll give you some sugarcane."

Everyone but Francis was amazed to see the elephant raise a heavy plank high in the air.

"See?" said Francis proudly. "Just what we needed—an elephant!"

After that, Francis and his elephant were allowed to help build the tree house.

The elephant hauled the heavy planks up from the beach.

And when work was over for the day, the elephant let Francis and his brothers ride on his back.

When the tree house was finally finished, the family threw a party. The elephant was the guest of honor.

"Without Francis and his elephant," said the father, "our new home might never have been built."

The elephant raised his trunk, as though to say, "Thank you."

Then Francis proudly gave his elephant the sweetest and best piece of sugarcane he could find.

Now Ireland, as you may know, is a green and lovely land. There's many a thousand Irishmen there, in every valley and town.

But there are others in Ireland, too, who make their homes snug

underground. You may not see one of them from New Year's Eve to year's end. But they are there, make no mistake. They're the Little People, the leprechauns.

A canny lot of wee folk are they, dressed in their suits of green. And many's the crock of gold they have miserly hidden away. But will they share it with human folk? They'll give you a trick instead!

Take the case of Darby O'Gill, which happened not long ago:

Darby was chasing his horse one night. The skittish mare led him across the sloping meadow and off toward the mountain beyond.

Now Darby knew as well as the next what dangers that mountain held. For it had the name of Knocknasheega, the hill of fairy folk.

And sure enough, elfin music seemed to rise up from the place. Darby heard it plain enough. It came from an open well. And a strange sort of light seemed to rise from there too.

Well, Darby was a man with his share of wonder. He bent over to peek down the hole.

As he did so, the fairy music grew wilder. Darby heard his horse give one strange, wild neigh. Then she pushed him, and he tumbled down that well!

When he awoke from his fall, he was flat on his back, lying on the floor of a cave.

Suddenly—*spang!*—wee men appeared around him.

Darby waved his stick.

"You wicked little creatures!" he cried.

"Watch your stick!" cried one of the leprechauns. And Darby's own trusty blackthorn flew out of his hands and beat its master's head!

"Come on," said another leprechaun. "We'll take you to our king."

Darby had nothing better to do, so he followed the little men. Many were the wonderful sights he saw in those caves deep underground. He saw leprechauns shoveling crocks full of gold. He saw others cobbling small fairy shoes.

And at last, in the Throne Room, a giant cave aglow with a light of its own, he came to the source of the fairy music. High on a golden throne sat King Brian. He was playing tiny bagpipes with might and main, and dancing around him were his green-coated men.

"Well, Darby O'Gill!" cried the Little People's king, laying aside his pipes. "I'm pleased and delighted to see you!"

"Thank you, sir," Darby said.

"Sit down," said the king, and waved his hand at a chest by the foot of his throne.

"Drop the lid, man," he said, as Darby just stared. "It's only an old chest of jewels."

Darby closed the lid and sat down.

Then the king showed him treasures here and there, scattered about the room.

"I declare to my soul!" cried Darby O'Gill. "When I tell this at home, they'll never believe me."

"Oh, you'll not do that, Darby," said the king with a smile. "Once you're here, there's no going back, you know."

"But I've got to go back!" cried Darby.

"Ah, no," said the little king. "You can say good-bye to the tears and the troubles of the world outside. There's nothing but fun and dancing here. Be a good lad now and give us a tune."

"Well," said Darby, with a glint in his eye, "I'm no great hand with the pipes or harp. But give me my old fiddle, and I can play you a tune worth going a mile o'ground to hear."

"Grand, grand," said Brian the King.

"But I'll have to go home," said Darby O'Gill. "To get the fiddle, you see."

"None of your tricks," said King Brian sternly. "I said you were here to stay."

He gave a snap of his fingers, and a fine old fiddle and its bow dropped into Darby's hands.

"Go ahead," said King Brian. "Give us a good one."

Darby tucked the fiddle under his chin and tried a chord or two. They sounded so magnificent that a bold plan came to him.

"I'll play you the Fox Chase," said Darby O'Gill. For he knew that the Little People loved both the dance and the hunt. They could not resist them at all.

Well, he played the gathering of the huntsmen and the hounds, and the start of the hunt.

"Off we go!" cried Darby, tapping his foot.
And the little men started to dance.

He played them the long, lone sound of the horn and the fine, fast music of the chase. You could hear the hounds baying and the riders galloping.

Soon the Little People were racing off to mount their white horses. With the king at their head, they circled the cave, while Darby fiddled the baying of a hound.

"Tallyho!" cried the king, with a crack of his whip. And the mountainside opened before him.

Then the moonlight flooded in, dazzling Darby's eyes. But he kept on fiddling as never before. And out streamed the king, with his hunters behind him, toward the night sky filled with stars.

When Darby was alone in the cave, he laid down the fiddle and started after them. But all of a sudden he thought of the chest of jewels beside the throne.

Back he went, and he lifted the lid and began to stuff his pockets with jewels.

A strange grating sound made him turn his head. The mountainside was closing again! Darby reached for one last handful of jewels. But there was not a moment to lose! So he raced for the opening, narrowed now to a crack in the mountainside.

Out he dove headfirst. And as he sprawled in the night-chilled grass, the mountain behind him closed with a crash. He shuddered at his narrow escape!

Then his hand went to his jewel-crammed pocket. Not a thing was there. Deeper he dug. Still only cloth. And then, at the bottom, he found a hole. As he had fled from the cave, all the jewels had trickled out!

So that was how it came about that Darby O'Gill came back to his home from a night with the Little People, with not a glint of treasure to show.

There were even those who doubted his word. But you and I understand.

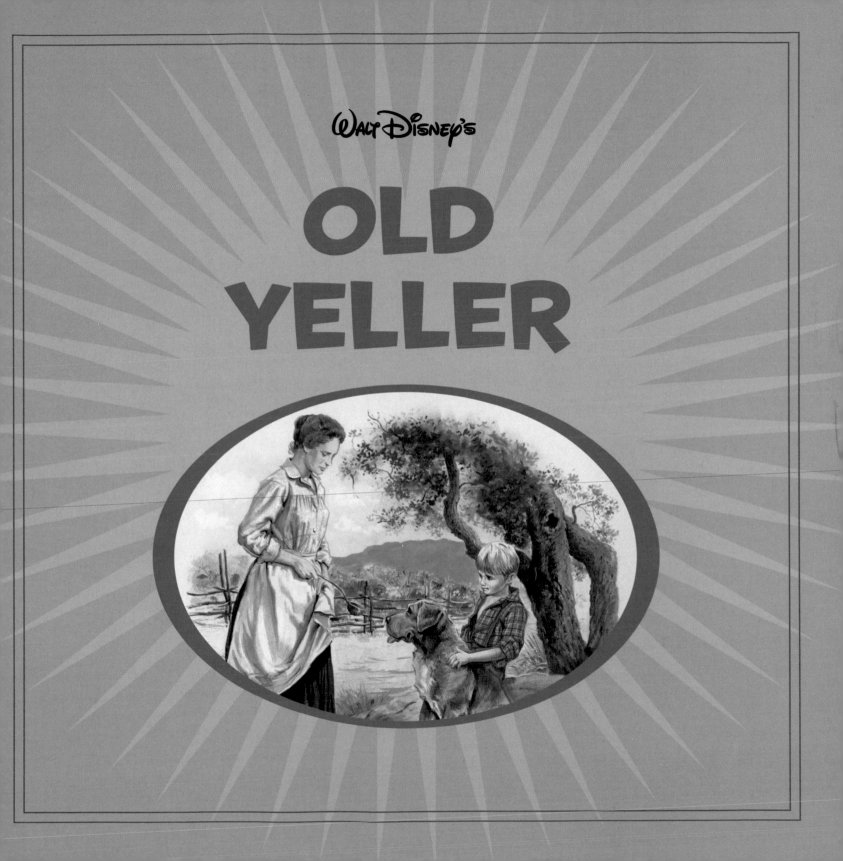

Nobody knew where Old Yeller came from. He just turned up one day at the Coates cabin, sniffing and wagging his tail.

The Coates boys, Arliss and Travis, looked him over. Not that he was much to look at. He was big and clumsy and yellow in color.

He was full of tricks, too. Whenever anyone picked up a stick or a stone, Old Yeller threw himself on the ground. He rolled around, howling and yowling worse than a wildcat.

And he had to be watched. If he wasn't, he'd steal a person blind. Why, he could snatch a whole side of meat as slick as you please.

Old Yeller and Arliss took to each other right off. But Mrs. Coates wasn't sure if they should keep the dog. "If your papa was here, he'd know what to do," she said.

But Mr. Coates was miles away, selling their steers in Abilene. He wouldn't be back for months. So Mrs. Coates told Arliss that Old Yeller could stay for the time being.

Whooping and hollering, Arliss ran for the pond, with Old Yeller right behind him.

Standing still, Old Yeller looked as though he couldn't walk without falling over his own feet. But when he started running, he was like a streak of lightning greased with hot bear oil. He was swift and sure and a sight to see.

He was so fast that he once caught a good-sized catfish in the pond for Arliss. Another time, he helped Travis drive some thieving raccoons out of the corn patch. And he was a wonder at herding cows or hogs.

Then one day, Arliss did something he shouldn't have and got himself into real trouble. He caught a bear cub by the leg. And he wouldn't let go, not even when the big old mother bear came charging at him, snarling and growling.

Suddenly, from no place in particular, Old Yeller came bounding up. He tore right into that old bear.

And while Old Yeller fought the bear, Mrs. Coates and Travis came running and pulled Arliss away from the cub.

Soon the big bear had enough fighting and went running off through the brush with her cub. After he saw that Arliss was safe, Old Yeller wagged his tail.

"Oh, you crazy, wonderful old dog!" Mrs. Coates cried. Now she was certain Old Yeller should stay.

But a few days later, a man came riding up to the cabin. His name was Sanderson, and he had lost a dog—a big yellow dog that was full of tricks. Old Yeller was his.

When Mr. Sanderson started to take Old Yeller away, Arliss shouted, "You can't have my dog!" Mrs. Coates and Travis had to hold him back.

Mr. Sanderson looked at Arliss and then got down from his horse. "Just a minute, young fellow," he said. "What's that in your pocket?" "A horned toad," Arliss said, and held it out.

"Finest horned toad I ever saw," Mr. Sanderson said. Right then and there, Mr. Sanderson offered to swap his dog for Arliss's toad...if Mrs. Coates threw in a good home-cooked meal.

Mrs. Coates smiled and nodded.

And so, Mr. Sanderson got a toad and a meal—and Arliss got Old Yeller.

"You're really my dog now, aren't you, boy?" Arliss said.

Old Yeller just wagged his tail and lay down in front of the fire. He knew he was there to stay.

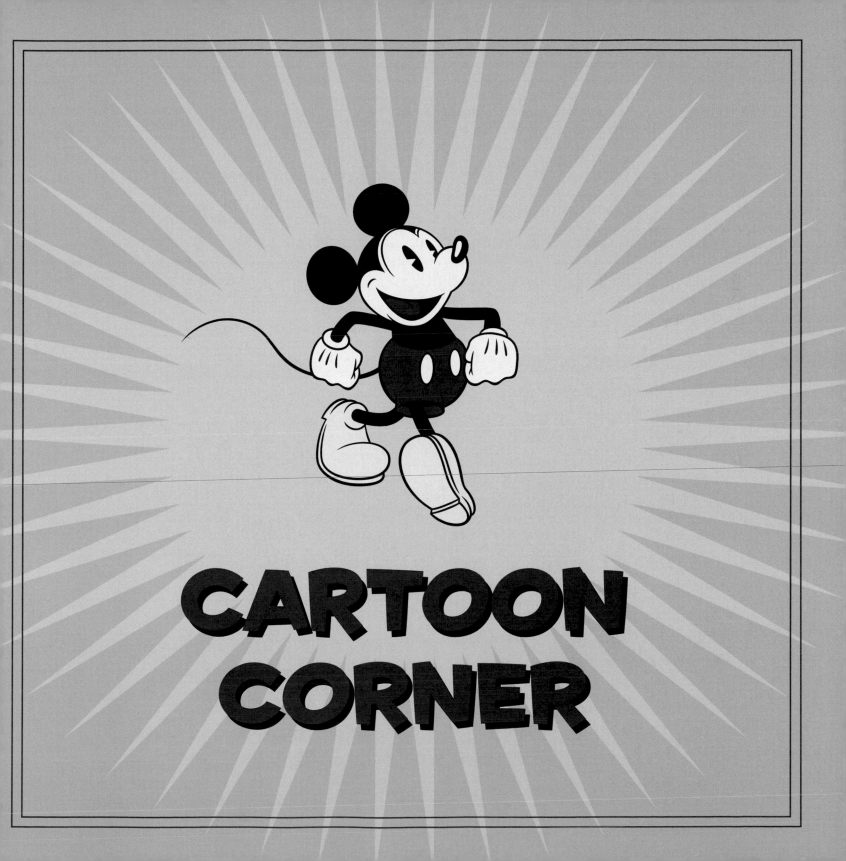

CARTOON
CORNER

Trouble, Inc.

Wilby Daniels was a typical American boy. He lived with his father, who was a mailman, and his mother and a younger brother in an attractive frame house in a small town called Springfield.

Wilby wasn't too tall or too short, too fat or too skinny. He wasn't exactly handsome, yet he was no monster, either. He did fairly well in school, and he liked to eat and talk on the telephone and play baseball.

All in all, Wilby was just an average teenager—except for one thing. He had an exceptional talent for getting into trouble.

Wilby could hit what seemed to be a winning home run, only to have the ball curve foul at the last minute and crash through the window of the principal's office. He could dress up in his best for a date with Allison D'Allessio, the pretty girl who lived next door, and then fall headlong into a mud puddle on the way to her house.

Once Wilby, with the assistance of his eight-year-old brother, Moochie, built a missile interceptor in the basement of his house. As he and Moochie were working on the contraption, the rocket fired prematurely, belching clouds of smoke. No one was hurt, but the blast did a lot of damage to the house.

Unfortunately Mr. Daniels was at home on vacation from his mail delivery job and witnessed the accident.

"Wilby!" he stormed. "This is the end. Your allowance is cut off. You won't get a penny until all the repairs are paid for. Understand?"

"Yes, sir," Wilby said sadly.

"And please try to stay out of trouble," Mr. Daniels pleaded. "Just for a little while. *Please!*"

Wilby did try and, for a few days, all went well. Then along came the shaggy dog, and trouble of a kind Wilby wouldn't have thought possible descended.

It began the afternoon Dr. Mikhail Valasky and his seventeen-year-old daughter, Franceska, moved into the old Coverly mansion directly across the street from the Daniels family.

Just about everybody in town had heard of the Valaskys. The *Gazette* had been carrying items for weeks about the distinguished European who was coming to take over the post of curator of the County Museum.

On this particular afternoon, Wilby was out in front of his home, discussing the little matter of a seven-dollar debt with Buzz Miller.

"How about forking over that money, Buzz," Wilby said. "I need it. Pop's still got me off my allowance."

Buzz lolled back lazily in the bucket seat of his flashy hot rod. He was a year older than Wilby and considered himself a man of the world.

"Sorry, Wilby, old boy," Buzz said. "But I can't part with those seven skins right now. I've got a date with Allison D'Allessio. I may take her to the Old Mill or the Purple Pad. Money is necessary to oil the wheels of romance, you know."

"Look," Wilby said angrily. "I'm tired of financing your romances. I'd like to take Allison out, myself."

Buzz laughed.

"And fall into another mud puddle?" he said. "Why don't you wait till you grow up, Junior, and leave affairs of the heart to us older men."

Wilby was getting madder by the second.

"I'm big enough and old enough to take care of the likes of you," he said. "And for two pins I'd . . ."

But Wilby never got to finish his sentence for, at that moment, a handsome convertible car of foreign make rolled into view along Elm Street, its radio blaring music. The car was driven by a young girl. Beside her was a distinguished middle-aged gentleman. And alone in the back seat was an enormous shaggy dog.

The dog had a tremendous white coat. His hair was so long that it hung over his face like a tangled floor mop. It's a wonder the poor animal could even see!

But neither Wilby nor Buzz paid much attention to the shaggy dog or to the dignified gentleman. Their eyes were on the girl behind the steering wheel.

She was so pretty that Wilby and Buzz could only stare, their argument forgotten.

"Wow!" Buzz gasped. "What a girl!"

Following along behind the foreign car was a heavily loaded moving van. It was only when the car and van turned up the driveway to the Coverly mansion that Wilby realized that the strangers were, without doubt, Dr. Mikhail Valasky and his daughter, Franceska.

"Franceska," Wilby murmured aloud. "It must be."

"What?" Buzz asked.

"She must be the daughter of the museum man . . . *Franceska!* What a beautiful name!"

"What a beautiful dame," Buzz replied.

The procession pulled to a stop alongside the gray stone mansion.

And, as Wilby and Buzz watched, Franceska emerged gracefully from the car, followed by Dr. Valasky and the shaggy dog. The girl bent down, gave the dog a loving caress, and entered the house.

Then a strange thing happened.

The shaggy dog immediately sped down the drive and raced across the street straight for Wilby. He charged up to the boy, wagging his tail and making shrill whining sounds. It was as if the dog had found a long lost friend.

Disappearance

Wilby was startled by the dog's friendly greeting.

"Well, well," he said. "He likes me."

"You can have him," Buzz said. "I'll take the mam'selle who owns him. I wish I could meet her."

Wilby patted the shaggy dog's head.

"You shouldn't run across the street like that, pal," he said. "You might get hit by a car."

"Hey, that's right," Buzz said. "It's dangerous for him to be loose. I'd better take him back to her. She'll be worrying about him."

Buzz vaulted out of his hot rod.

"Now just a minute, wise guy," Wilby said. "The dog came to me. I'll return him."

Buzz sighed. "All right. We'll both take him back."

The shaggy dog stayed close to Wilby as the two boys went up the drive to the mansion. A stiff-faced butler opened the door at their knock.

"You wish to see someone?" he asked.

"We brought back the young lady's dog," Buzz said.

Just then Franceska appeared in the hall.

"Who is it, Stefano?" she asked.

"Two young men have returned Chiffon, mademoiselle," the butler said. The girl came to the door and Wilby's head swam. She was even more beautiful close up.

"Your dog was running away and we caught him," Buzz said glibly. "It was quite a job."

"Chiffon running away?" the girl said. "That's odd. He's never done that before. But thank you both for bringing him back. . . . My name is Franceska Valasky."

"I'm Buzz Miller," Buzz said. "It's a real pleasure to know you, Miss Valasky. Welcome to Springfield."

"And I'm Wilby Daniels," Wilby said. He tried vainly to think of something that would top Buzz. "I . . . I live right across the street."

"Then we're neighbors," Franceska said. "Won't you come in? I'd like you to meet my father."

The girl took hold of Chiffon's collar and led the way to the living room. Movers were carrying in many crates and pictures and statues.

"Please excuse the disorder," Franceska said. "We've just arrived, you know. . . . Do sit down."

Wilby had just lowered himself to a sofa when Chiffon pulled away from Franceska. The huge dog made a beeline for Wilby and tried to climb up in his lap, almost smothering him.

"Well," Franceska said with a laugh. "I've never seen Chiffon take such a fancy to anyone before."

"Sure is friendly!" Wilby gasped. "What kind is he?"

"A Bratislavian sheepdog," Franceska said. "A very rare breed. They were popular with the Borgias.

"The Borgias had a habit of poisoning people during the Dark Ages in Italy," she went on. "And it's claimed they dabbled in sorcery and black magic. You've heard of them, of course."

"Of course," Buzz said. "I have—but I don't know about Wilby."

At that moment Dr. Valasky came into the room, and Franceska introduced the boys to him.

"How do you do, gentlemen?" Dr. Valasky said. He was carrying a leather case. "I wonder if you would deliver these Orsini artifacts to Dr. Howard at the museum, Franceska. He's waiting for them. Perhaps the young men can tell you how to get there."

"Better than that, sir," Buzz said. "I'll drive her to the museum. My car's outside."

"Yes," Wilby said. "We'll both take her."

He ignored the murderous look Buzz sent him.

"How nice," Franceska said. "Shall we go then?"

When they left the house, the shaggy dog tried to follow after Wilby but Franceska closed the door.

"You stay home, Chiffon," she said.

Wilby heard Chiffon whine and he felt sorry for him. Wilby loved dogs. He'd always wanted to own one. But that was impossible because of his father. Mr. Daniels had a deep-rooted hatred of all canines.

"No dog will ever live in my house," he'd said more than once. "I've had enough of 'em yelping and snapping at me while I'm delivering mail. I'll make any mutt that trespasses on my property sorry!"

The drive across town in Buzz's hot rod was maddening to Wilby. Not only was he forced to ride alone in the back, but Buzz kept up such a steady flow of talk with Franceska that Wilby couldn't get in a word.

But worse was to come when they entered the museum. Wilby paused for a moment to examine an exhibit of prehistoric animals. When he turned around, Buzz and Franceska were nowhere to be seen.

Black Magic

It was just like Buzz to pull a sneaky trick like that and take Franceska off, Wilby thought.

He began searching through room after room, determined to find them. He came to a doorway over which was lettered: RENAISSANCE PERIOD. He went in. The place was eerily lighted. Wax figures garbed in clothes of the Middle Ages lined the walls.

"Buzz?" Wilby called. "Franceska?"

A man came from behind a glass case so suddenly that Wilby jumped. The man was elderly and stooped.

"Professor Plumcutt!" Wilby cried, recognizing him. "Gosh, you scared me."

Professor Plumcutt came closer, staring.

"Why, it's Wilby Daniels," he said. "Haven't seen you since you used to deliver my paper. What are you doing here, boy?"

"Looking for two friends of mine," Wilby said. "They were going to Dr. Howard's office."

"That's the other way then," the professor said. "How do you like my display of the Age of Sorcery? Never have we had such an exhibit. Every practitioner of black magic is represented—witches, sorcerers, charlatans . . . all of them."

Wilby glanced uneasily around him. He noticed for the first time the evil expressions on the wax faces.

"It's . . . it's fine, Professor," he said.

"The best one of all is Lucretia Borgia here."

The professor gestured to the figure of a sinister woman. *Borgia.* There was that name again.

"Delightful days when the Borgias lived," Professor Plumcutt went on. "Sorcery and witchcraft were at their heights. Even shape-shifting."

"Shape-shifting?" Wilby said. "What's that?"

"Why, the medieval art of borrowing someone else's body to live in for a while. You've heard of human beings turned into foxes and cats and other creatures, haven't you?"

"You don't believe in that stuff, do you, Professor?" Wilby asked nervously. The professor's eyes glittered.

"Today people laugh at such things. But there are times during dark and lonely nights when something inside of us begins to stir. Who is to say that it's not an awakening of ancient fears and beliefs? Who is to say that some day I—or you, Wilby—might not fall under an evil spell?"

Wilby shivered. He had to get out of there.

The professor took a tray of jeweled objects from a glass case.

"Here is some of the jewelry worn by the Borgias," he said. "Perhaps some mystic power still remains in these rings and bracelets and necklaces. Intriguing thought, eh, my boy?"

"I guess so," Wilby said. "I must be going, Professor. Nice to have seen you."

He turned quickly to head for the door. As he did, his arm hit the tray in Professor Plumcutt's hands. The tray crashed to the floor, scattering the jewelry.

"I'm sorry," Wilby said. "I'll help pick them up."

"No . . . no!" the professor cried. "I'd better handle these. Go along, Wilby. Just go along."

Wilby was only too happy to obey.

There was still no sign of Buzz and Franceska anywhere, and when he got outside the museum, Buzz's car was gone. Now he'd have to walk.

It was almost dinnertime when Wilby got home.

His disposition wasn't improved any by his father ordering him to the basement after dinner. There was still plenty of cleaning up to be done from the rocket explosion.

Wilby was dumping a load of junk into a box when he noticed a faint glow coming from the bottom of one of his trouser legs. He bent down to investigate and found in the cuff a delicately fashioned ring of gold.

"It must have fallen there when I knocked over that tray at the museum," he muttered.

Wilby held up the ring to the light and examined it. There were words engraved on the band.

"*In canis corpore, transmuto,*" he read. "Hey, that's Latin. Wonder what it means. *Canis,* that's dog, I think. *In canis* . . . into dog . . . *corpore, transmuto* . . . I don't get that part."

He slipped the ring on the third finger of his left hand. It fit perfectly.

Suddenly, Wilby heard the far-away sounds of a stringed instrument, then the distant rumble of thunder. He began to feel very strange.

He saw in bewilderment that something was happening to his hand. The fingers were becoming stubby. The hair on his head seemed to be growing longer. It was falling down over his eyes.

In alarm, he rushed over to where a cracked full-length mirror leaned against the basement wall. He stared at his reflection.

It took him a full minute to realize the terrible thing that had happened. Inside he was still Wilby Daniels. But outside he had turned into—a shaggy dog!

The Mystic Spell

No! Wilby thought. It couldn't be. There was some mistake. He was just having a dream about that shape-shifting stuff old Professor Plumcutt had mentioned. People didn't turn into dogs.

Yet no matter how he moved and grimaced in front of the mirror, the reflected image remained the same. The Wilby Daniels he knew was gone and in his place was Franceska's shaggy dog—or a dog very like him!

Suddenly, Wilby heard his mother call from upstairs in the kitchen.

"Better come up soon, Wilby! You must be tired!"

Wilby scuttled under the cellar stairs. He couldn't let her see him.

"Wilby!" his mother called again. "Did you hear what I said?"

"Yes, Mom," Wilby said. "I'll be up in a while."

He was startled at the gruffness of his voice.

"Are you getting a cold, dear?" his mother asked. "You sound hoarse.

I'll bring you a sweater in a minute."

"No . . . no!" Wilby said frantically. "I have a coat on."

He had a coat on, all right—a great big white shaggy coat! Glancing down at himself, Wilby noticed that the ring he'd put on his finger now encircled a toe of his left front paw.

The Borgia ring! That's what had done this terrible thing to him. By repeating those Latin words he must have brought on an ancient curse.

He'd have to go and see Professor Plumcutt at once. Maybe the professor would know how to break the strange spell.

Wilby waited until he heard his mother go to the front of the house. Then he bounded up the cellar steps and out the back door. Professor Plumcutt might still be at the museum. He'd try there first.

To save time, Wilby took a shortcut that led him right by the Coverly mansion. A side window was open and he heard Franceska's sweet voice.

"Have you seen Chiffon, Father?" Franceska said. "He was lying right at my feet a few minutes ago. Now he's gone. I didn't see him leave. I can't understand it."

Well, that made one thing pretty clear, Wilby thought. When he'd turned into a shaggy dog, Chiffon had vanished. That seemed to mean that he was in Chiffon's body. It meant, too, that he now belonged to the beautiful Franceska!

It seemed perfectly natural to Wilby to run on four legs. In fact, he almost liked it. And when a spaniel came racing after him, barking, Wilby let out a ferocious growl.

"Beat it, mutt!" he yelled. "Go chase your tail!"

The human voice coming from a dog was too much for the spaniel. It fled in terror.

Wilby found a side door of the museum open. He slipped in and padded down a corridor to the Renaissance Room. He was in luck. Professor Plumcutt was still there, working.

"Professor," Wilby said, "I've got to talk to you."

The professor looked up from his work.

"Dogs aren't allowed in here," he said.

"But I'm not a dog. I'm Wilby Daniels."

The professor adjusted his glasses. "Well, bless my soul! Are you really? How did you manage it?"

He seemed much more delighted than surprised.

Wilby held up his left paw.

"I think this ring did it. I found it in the cuff of my pants. And I read the inscription."

"The Borgia ring! I've been looking all over for it." Professor Plumcutt reached out and removed the ring. "Thanks for returning it.

Now, run along. I'm very busy," he said.

"But what about me?" Wilby asked. "You've got to help me, Professor. I don't want to be a dog."

"Good gracious, Wilby," Professor Plumcutt said. "I don't know how to break magic charms. And shape-shifting ones are the hardest of all."

"Surely something can be done," Wilby said.

"Well," the professor said slowly, "in the olden days a feat of heroism, like rescuing a maiden in distress, sometimes worked. But I'm afraid you'll just have to wait and see. Some spells come and go like headaches. . . . Now, if you'll excuse me, my boy . . . er . . . my dog."

Wilby padded slowly out of the museum, his tail drooping. Now what was he going to do? If he went home he might get hurt. His father had threatened to use his shotgun on any dog found in the house or on the grounds.

Yet there was no other place to spend the night. He'd just have to try and keep out of sight.

Wilby sneaked up to his house. He made sure his father and mother were in the living room. Then he eased in through the back door and ran upstairs to the room he shared with his younger brother, Moochie.

Moochie was in bed and asleep. Moving carefully so as not to awaken him, Wilby got out his pajamas. It was quite a struggle to pull them on. And he found it was even more difficult to brush his teeth. They were so much bigger than they used to be.

Finally, Wilby crawled into bed and pulled the covers over himself. Maybe by morning the spell would have worn off. He was so tired that he fell asleep almost instantly.

Pursuit

Wilby was awakened the next morning by the sound of his brother's voice.

"Get up, Wilby," Moochie said. "Pop just yelled that breakfast is ready."

Wilby threw back the covers and opened his eyes. He heard Moochie gasp.

"How did you get in here?" Moochie asked.

"I happen to live here," Wilby said, yawning.

"But you can't! You're a dog!" Moochie exclaimed.

A shudder passed through Wilby. He leaped out of bed and rushed to the mirror. His shaggy, doggy image looked back at him. The spell was still on him.

Pacing dejectedly on all fours, Wilby told his brother about the dreadful thing that had happened. Far from being upset, Moochie was overjoyed.

"Oh, boy!" he cried. "I've always wanted a dog. I'll be good to you, Wilby. I'll get you the best bones and dust you with flea powder. . . . I only hope Pop won't find you."

Wilby stiffened. His father!

"Hurry down to breakfast, Moochie," Wilby said. "I can't show myself. Make some excuse for me."

"I'll tell them you aren't hungry," Moochie said.

"Hungry!" Wilby moaned. "I'm starved."

After Moochie had gone, Wilby pulled off his pajamas. He'd have to skip trying to get anything to eat. It would be too risky. But the smell of bacon wafting upstairs was too much. Maybe he could slip into the kitchen unobserved and get something.

His father and mother and Moochie were in the dining room having their cereal when Wilby reached the bottom of the stairs. Moving quietly, he sneaked into the kitchen. The first thing he saw was a platter of bacon his mother had left on the stove to keep warm.

He stood on his hind legs and attacked the crunchy bacon. Just as he was reaching for one last delicious morsel, the swinging door opened and his father appeared.

Mr. Daniels' eyes bulged. "A dog!" he yelled.

Wilby didn't loiter. He hit the kitchen screen door at top speed, blasted it open, and catapulted out into the yard.

"My gun!" he heard his father shout. "I'll teach that mangy cur a lesson!"

A moment later, just as Wilby dived for cover behind the garbage, the shotgun blasted.

"You fleabag!" Mr. Daniels yelled. "If you ever come near here again, I'll fill you full of buckshot!"

Unharmed, but a nervous wreck, Wilby kept running. He sure was in hot water now. The only safe haven would be in Chiffon's home.

Stefano, the butler, heard Wilby whining at the back door of the Coverly mansion and let him in.

"Miss Franceska!" he called. "It is Chiffon."

Franceska appeared and threw her arms around what she thought was her dog.

"You bad dog. Where have you been all night? I've been worried sick."

Wilby wriggled closer to the girl and put his head next to hers. Hey, he thought, this wasn't too bad. If only Buzz could see him now. He gave Franceska a kiss on the cheek.

"You're a rogue," she said. "But I love you."

Stefano put some dog food in a bowl. Wilby thought the stuff tasted like moldy hay but he forced himself to eat it because Franceska was watching.

"Now I must go shopping," Franceska said. "I need a new dress for the dance tonight."

The country club dance, Wilby thought. It was tonight. And here he was—a dog!

"Buzz Miller is taking me," Franceska said.

Wilby growled and showed his teeth.

"So you don't like him, Chiffon. I suppose you think that Wilby Daniels is nicer."

Wilby thumped his tail hard against the floor.

"They're both nice boys," Franceska said. "Now while I'm gone, you stay in the house. No more wandering."

Wilby prowled around the mansion after Franceska left. The idea of Buzz dating her drove him wild. If he could only get his real body back and go to the dance, he'd show Buzz a thing or two.

Wilby had finally settled down on a soft rug in Dr. Valasky's upstairs study when Stefano showed in a caller. Dr. Valasky immediately closed and locked the door.

"You have the sketches, Mr. Thurm?" he asked.

Mr. Thurm had a hard, cruel face and Wilby didn't like him. Thurm opened his briefcase and dropped some papers on the desk.

"Of course, I have them," he said.

Dr. Valasky bent over the papers.

"Excellent," he said. "They seem to be just what we want. When will they be completed?"

"With luck I will have the final detail of Section Thirty-two tomorrow," Thurm said. He looked around cautiously. "You are sure nobody suspects?"

"The plan is foolproof," Dr. Valasky said. "Even my daughter knows nothing."

The hard-faced man didn't stay long. When he left, Wilby followed him down the stairs. He couldn't help but wonder what all the secrecy was about.

Then all speculation was wiped from Wilby's mind as he heard once again the faraway sounds of a stringed instrument. It was followed by a peal of thunder.

Wilby felt himself shaking. He put out a paw to steady himself. In amazement he saw that his toes had lengthened into fingers, and his heavy coat of hair was fast disappearing.

He leaped up and stared into the hall mirror. He could scarcely believe his eyes. The shaggy dog was gone. He was the real Wilby Daniels again.

Wilby made for the front door. Just as he opened it, he saw Chiffon appear in the hall behind him.

"Chiffon," Wilby said, "I've had enough of a dog's life. It's all yours from now on."

Once outside, he broke into a run. He felt like yelling at the top of his lungs. Now he could go home! Now he could go to the dance!

The Chase

Wearing a white jacket and dark slacks, Wilby did attend the dance that night. He was so happy to go that he didn't even object when Buzz proposed that they team up and take Allison D'Allessio and Franceska. Buzz was in trouble. He'd asked *both* girls to the dance.

But Wilby's hopes that his troubles were over at last were shattered.

Midway through the evening, he was standing by himself at one end of the dance hall, waiting for Franceska, who had gone to the powder room. The lights dimmed and the orchestra began playing a waltz.

Wilby heard the strumming of a stringed instrument. At first he thought the sound came from the orchestra—until strands of long hair began falling down over his eyes. Then he knew that he was turning into a shaggy dog again!

Couples were now on the floor. Beyond them, Wilby saw Franceska coming toward him. He had to get away!

He plunged across the crowded dance floor, making for an open doorway that led to the outside. He had no time to pick his course. His massive bulk slammed into dancing couples, scattering them like ten-pins. Girls screamed and the boys shouted. Through the bedlam, Wilby heard Franceska's voice.

"It's Chiffon! Catch him, Buzz! Catch him!"

Somebody tried to grab Wilby by the collar but he wrenched himself free and sped out the door into the cool darkness of the night. A quick glance over his shoulder told him that Buzz and a crowd of fellows were following in hot pursuit.

"All right," Wilby growled. "I'll give you a run for your money."

Keeping just ahead of his pursuers, Wilby led the pack of boys back and forth across the golf course.

When he decided that they'd had enough, he disappeared into the woods and returned to town.

Going home would mean risking his father's shotgun. He'd have to spend the night at Franceska's.

When he arrived, Stefano let him in.

"You miserable beast," the butler said. "You were supposed to stay locked up here in the kitchen. I don't know how you got out."

Stefano was preparing coffee and a sandwich, apparently for Dr. Valasky. While his back was turned, Wilby went to the small writing room in the front of the house where he knew there was a telephone. He shoved the door closed, then lifted the phone off its cradle with his teeth. He found it a lot easier to dial with a toenail than he'd imagined.

"Hello, Mom," Wilby said when he heard his mother answer. "Is it okay if I stay at Buzz's tonight?"

"I guess so, dear," his mother said. "Did you have fun at the dance?"

"It was a real riot," Wilby said. "Thanks, Mom."

He hated to mislead his mother, yet he couldn't have her sitting up all night, worrying about him.

Wilby left the room and was crossing the hall when Franceska came in the front door. Buzz was with her. Wilby noticed with pleasure that Buzz was a mess. His coat and slacks were stained and torn, and there was a scratch on his cheek.

"Chiffon!" Franceska cried. "I'm ashamed of you! You almost wrecked the dance, you bad dog!"

"Look what he did to me," Buzz said.

"I'm sorry about that, Buzz," Franceska replied.

"And another thing," Buzz went on. "Your friend, Wilby—who you seemed to like dancing with—where was he when we were chasing this animated mop over hill and dale? He just vanished, that's all."

"It *is* strange about Wilby," Franceska said.

"Well, let's forget all that," Buzz said. He took Franceska's hands. "Let's talk about us. You know, there's something about you, Franceska, that's really wonderful. Your eyes . . . your . . ."

Suddenly, Wilby gave a ferocious growl and advanced on Buzz, showing his teeth and snarling. Buzz let go of Franceska's hands and backed toward the door.

"I don't think your dog likes me," he said. "Maybe I'd better go. . . . Good night."

As the door closed behind Buzz, Wilby looked up at Franceska and wagged his tail.

"Oh, no, you can't make up to me," she said. "You're getting to be a real problem, Chiffon."

Just then, Stefano came from the kitchen carrying a tray with a pot of coffee and a sandwich.

"Stefano," Franceska said, "I distinctly told you to keep Chiffon locked up tonight."

"I put him in the kitchen and turned the key in the lock, mademoiselle," the butler said. "Still he escaped."

"See that he doesn't again. Good night."

Franceska went up the stairs without another look at Wilby.

"Come along with me," the butler said to Wilby. "I'm taking no chances on you."

When Stefano opened the door to Dr. Valasky's study, Wilby went in ahead of him. He stretched out on the soft rug near the desk and sighed. It had been quite an evening, all in all. But the best part had been scaring Buzz.

Dr. Valasky was seated at his desk, and the butler put the tray down in front of him.

"Just a minute, Stefano," Dr. Valasky said. "I have a few things to talk over with you."

"Yes, sir."

"I've heard from Thurm again," Dr. Valasky said. His voice was low. "He's been transferred to Section Thirty-two at the missile plant. He'll have the components here late tomorrow afternoon."

"Ah," Stefano said.

Wilby raised his shaggy head. What was all this whispered stuff about anyway?

"It means that the complete mechanism of the undersea hydrogen missile will finally be in our hands," Dr. Valasky went on. "We must get it out of the country immediately. And that's where you come in, Stefano."

"Yes, sir," the butler said.

"When Thurm delivers the components you will take them to my office at the museum and place them in the special containers in the case with the Etruscan fossils. You will then see that the case is shipped on the midnight plane—ostensibly to the museum in Rome. Our contact there will do the rest."

"But what if the authorities examine the case?"

"Even so," Dr. Valasky said with a smile, "I doubt if they will tamper with such a priceless collection."

Wilby was numb with shock. No wonder the stranger named Thurm had acted so mysteriously that morning. He and Stefano and Dr. Valasky were—*spies!*

He'd have to do something to stop them, Wilby thought desperately. As soon as everything quieted down for the night he'd escape from the house and somehow warn the police.

But Wilby was unable to carry out his plan. For when Stefano left the study, Dr. Valasky went with him and the dog started to follow.

"Chiffon has been a nuisance, sir," the butler said. "I think we should lock him in here for the night."

"Good idea," Dr. Valasky replied.

The door closed and to his horror, Wilby heard the click of metal as the key was turned from the outside.

He was trapped.

Getaway

It was a terrible night for Wilby. He prowled endlessly around the room, trying to find some way out. Finally, exhausted, he sank down and slept.

He was still dozing when Stefano came in the next morning. The butler had a leash in his hands. He snapped it on Wilby's collar.

"I'm taking no chances with you running off," Stefano said. "Now come and get your breakfast."

Holding the leather loop at the end of the leash, the butler led Wilby down to the kitchen. Wilby went meekly. The leash made escape much more difficult, but he'd have to make a break for it just the same.

The opportunity came as Stefano reached up on a shelf for a box of dog food. With a sudden jerk, Wilby yanked the leash from Stefano's grasp. Then he pushed the screen door open and rushed outside.

"Come back here!" Stefano yelled.

Pursued by the butler, Wilby rounded the corner of the mansion and bounded down the driveway toward his own home. Moochie was outside by the garage. Wilby headed for his brother, dragging the leash behind him.

"Moochie!" he called. He kept his voice low so the approaching butler wouldn't hear him.

"Wilby!" Moochie cried. "You're a dog again. Great!"

"Get this," Wilby said, panting. "There are a bunch of spies across the street. They're stealing something called Section Thirty-two from the missile plant. Tell Pop . . . tell the police . . ."

Stefano had almost caught up to him now, and Wilby started running again. He swerved toward the D'Allessios' house. Suddenly the loop at the end of the leash caught on a tree root, and Wilby was brought up short. Before he could free himself, Stefano managed to grab the leash.

"You miserable creature," the butler snarled. "I'm going to put an end to this unacceptable behavior for once and for all."

Wilby struggled to break free but it was useless. Stefano pulled him back to the kitchen. Once inside, the butler poured dog food into a bowl and added something to it from a small bottle.

Wilby ate what was put in front of him. The smart thing to do, he decided, was to be submissive and hope that Moochie would broadcast the warning. It was only after Wilby had eaten all the food that he noticed the label on the small bottle the butler had used. Printed on it were the words SLEEPING PILLS. He'd been doped!

Wilby felt himself getting groggy. Using all his willpower, he managed to drag himself up the stairs to Dr. Valasky's study. He'd just have to stay awake to listen for any new developments.

But he couldn't keep his eyes open. His shaggy head nodded and Wilby collapsed limply on the floor.

It was after five o'clock in the afternoon when he opened his eyes. Dr. Valasky was in the study. So was Mr. Thurm. Then Stefano came in.

"We're in serious trouble, Stefano," Wilby heard Dr. Valasky say. "Mr. Thurm was able to get the secret data he wanted. But there's been a leak somewhere. An investigation is going on at the missile plant."

The butler went pale. "An investigation!"

"Yes. Mr. Thurm fears he's under suspicion. We can't risk being picked up. We'll all have to clear out. . . . Is the boat ready?"

"Yes, sir," Stefano said. "Tied up at Walker's dock."

"Good. We'll leave immediately in Mr. Thurm's car. Tell my daughter she is going with us."

Excitement surged through Wilby. The investigation at the missile plant seemed to mean that Moochie must have tipped off the authorities. But would the police arrive before the spies escaped?

Franceska came to the doorway, with Stefano.

"What's this about going away?" she asked.

"We're leaving on a trip, Franceska," Dr. Valasky said. "There's no time to pack. Get into the car."

"But I have a date with Buzz Miller," Franceska said. "Anyway, you can't order me around like this. You're not my father. It's time to stop pretending. When you adopted me, I hoped you would be the kind of man my father was. But you aren't."

"Enough of that!" Dr. Valasky ordered.

He grasped Franceska by the arm and hurried her out. Thurm followed and so did Stefano.

"Chiffon!" Franceska cried. "We can't possibly leave Chiffon behind!"

"He stays here and good riddance," Dr. Valasky said.

Wilby sprang to his feet and with a growl he charged for the open doorway. From the hallway Stefano looked back and saw him coming. The butler slammed the door shut. Wilby crashed hard against it, striking his head.

Dazed by the impact, he reeled to one side. From beyond the closed door came the sound of feet pounding down the stairs. The spies were getting away and taking Franceska with them!

Desperately, Wilby seized the doorknob in his teeth and turned it.

The door opened, and Wilby shot down the staircase to the main floor like a furry cannonball. Through a side window he saw Dr. Valasky and the others piling into a long black sedan.

Wilby didn't bother with the front door. He sprang for the window and hurtled through it, taking the screen with him. He landed sprawled out on the grass. By the time he had picked himself up, the black car was speeding down the drive.

"Wilby!" he heard somebody yell. "Wilby!"

It was Moochie. He was coming across the lawn on the run.

"I told Pop and the police and the men at the missile plant about the spies," Moochie said, gasping. "At first they wouldn't believe me. But they're coming here to investigate."

"They'll be too late!" Wilby cried. "The spies have left. . . . If I only had a car."

"Look," Moochie said, pointing. "There's Buzz."

It was true. Buzz Miller had pulled his hot rod to a stop at the curb and was getting out. He was coming for his date with Franceska.

"Phone the police," Wilby said to Moochie. "Tell them to get to Walker's dock—fast!"

Then Wilby was on his way. Buzz saw him coming and his face went pale.

"Nice dog," he said nervously. "Nice dog."

Wilby whipped past him and with a leap landed in the front seat of the hot rod. He started the engine and by the time Buzz had turned around, the car was speeding down the street.

"Help!" Buzz yelled. "That mangy cur has taken my car! He's driving it!"

Wilby bent low over the steering wheel. Let Buzz scream his lungs out, he thought. Nothing mattered but getting to Walker's dock before the spies took to sea.

Wilby almost didn't make it. When he brought the hot rod to a skidding stop at the dock, the engines of the sleek forty-foot cruiser at the end of the pier were booming and the craft was getting underway.

Wilby was out of the car in a flash. On all fours he fairly flew along the rough planks of the dock. Thurm and Stefano were in the aft cockpit with Dr. Valasky at the wheel. The men were all facing forward. They were unaware of the fast-approaching shaggy dog. But Franceska saw him as she stood alone near the bow.

"Chiffon!" she cried.

Stefano turned. So did Thurm. So did Dr. Valasky.

At that moment Wilby left the dock in a tremendous leap. His massive body cleared the gap that had opened up between the cruiser and the pier. He landed squarely in the cockpit—with devastating results.

Thurm was knocked flat. Stefano was thrown heavily against Dr. Valasky. The cruiser veered abruptly and slammed headlong into a piling.

Wilby heard Franceska scream. Then he had a blurred impression of the girl being thrown overboard by the impact of the crash. When she came to the surface of the water she began thrashing about in a panic.

Wilby jumped in after her. Using a strong dog paddle, he reached the floundering girl. He grabbed her sweater with his teeth and headed for shore.

Wilby pulled Franceska up on land. She lay face down, gasping and sobbing. Wilby sank on his haunches, breathing hard. All of a sudden the music of stringed instruments came to his ears, followed by the boom of thunder. He stood up hastily. He was changing into his human shape again.

Moving quickly, he darted into the deep shadow cast by the pier, not wanting Franceska to see him. How could he ever explain his presence to her? When he looked back, he started in surprise. The girl was no longer alone. The real Chiffon had magically appeared and was there beside her.

Franceska had her arms around the shaggy dog, hugging him.

"Chiffon," she said. "Oh, Chiffon. You saved my life, you wonderful, beautiful dog!"

Then Wilby remembered what Professor Plumcutt had said. A magic spell could be broken by rescuing a maiden in distress. And he'd done just that. Now perhaps his troubles would be over.

In the distance he heard the sound of sirens. The police were coming. They'd take care of Dr. Valasky and Stefano and Thurm.

There was really no sense hanging around. No one would believe his story anyway.

Just before Wilby retreated into the darkness under the dock, he looked once again at Franceska and Chiffon. The girl's face was turned away from him as she clung to Chiffon. But Chiffon gazed right back at Wilby. And Wilby would have sworn that even with the long hair drooping over his face, the shaggy dog closed one eye in a wink.